A
PRESIDENTS DAY
CAROL

in Prose, Being a Ghost-Story of Presidents Day
in which One May Choose an Ending

ERIC M. HAMILTON

BRIEF
CONCEPTS

The author greatly appreciates your time in reading this work. Please consider leaving a review wherever you bought this book, or telling your friends about *A Presidents Day Carol*, to help spread the word.

Thank you for your support!

ISBN-13: 9798876866837

Other books by Eric M. Hamilton:

Presidents of the Uncanny States of America Series:
Franklin Pierce in Death of a Vice President
An Inconvenient Presidency

Short Stories:
It Came from the Lunchbox

Flash Fiction Collections:
Momentary Lapses into Sanity

To anyone who can take a joke.

NOTE

This book features an innovative
"choose your own ending" feature.
To avoid spoilers, the table of contents
is included at the end of this book.

Remember the days of old, Consider the years of all generations. Ask your father, and he will inform you; Your elders, and they will tell you.

MOSES

Human nature will not change. In any future great national trial, compared with the men of this, we shall have as weak and as strong, as silly and as wise, as bad and as good. Let us therefore study the incidents in this as philosophy to learn wisdom from and none of them as wrongs to be avenged.

ABRAHAM LINCOLN

If you hang around with losers, you become a loser.

DONALD TRUMP

1

Decency was dead to begin with.

There is much debate as to the exact moment decency died. Some mark the time of death as Election Day, November 2016. In truth, decency had long since kicked the bucket. Election Day was merely when everyone rummaged about for decency and, with a sudden dread, noticed it missing. Decency had been dead long before then, long before there were Republicans and Democrats, long before the founding of the Republic, long before there was even such a notion as the United States.

Regardless of when decency had died, it was certainly dead now, as dead as a compromise in Congress.

It was February 19th, 2017. A winter storm swept across the Atlantic Seaboard, and snow carpeted the nation's capital. Most of the population enjoyed their

Sunday off watching the snow settle from inside their cozy homes. The city and most government offices were barren in anticipation of the extended weekend bleeding into Monday. But one man was still working through the weekend and through the snowfall. He had only been sworn in as President of the United States a month before, but he did not let that prevent him from accomplishing his duty to his country.

"Have you heard this? It's quite incredible. Only a month into the job, and they've already given me my own holiday," Donald J. Trump said as the doors to the Oval Office opened. It did not matter who was entering. They certainly needed to know, whomever they were. "I truly am the greatest President there ever was, and the people, those glorious American people, agree. Look at these Twitter comments. There's thousands of them. Millions." Trump scrolled through a selections of tweets on his phone for demonstration.

It was Vice President Mike Pence who had entered. He sighed in the manner of an exhausted teacher correcting a child for the thousandth time. "Presidents Day didn't start this year. It's the celebration of George Washington's birthday as a federal holiday, but many states include Lincoln and other Presidents as well. Hence the name. There isn't even agreement over whether the holiday is for one or more Presidents. Different places put an apostrophe in different places or leave it out altogether. So the holiday—"

"I know that. Do you think I don't know that? Of course there were other Presidents Days, but the holiday has reached perfection with the greatest

President of them all. Excuse me," Trump said, tapping furiously on his phone. "I had something really important to tweet just now."

 Donald J. Trump @realDonaldTrump
Tomorrow is President's Day, my gift to you, the American people. Your welcome. #greatestPrez

"I've looked over your preliminary list of Supreme Court nominations," Pence said, getting to the point of his visit. "The Senate is not going to approve any of them."

"Not a problem," Donald Trump said without looking up from his phone. "I've come up with the perfect candidate for the Supreme Court. I can't believe I didn't think of it sooner."

Mike Pence waited a moment for Trump to continue, but he did not. After a long enough awkward silence, the Vice President said, "And who is it?"

"Me," said Donald.

"You?"

"Me," said Donald again, returning his focus to Pence. "If the American people love me as President, they'll love me as Supreme Court Justice. It's a no-brainer."

Pence pinched his nose and furrowed his brow. "You can't just nominate yourself to the Supreme Court. They're separate branches. Are you planning on resigning from the presidency?" Mike Pence asked that last question with a little more neediness than he intended to. Trump did not seem to notice.

"You're not the only one who's been studying," Trump said. "I did some of my own research, and President Howard Taft—nice guy, but definitely ate too much, over three hundred pounds, not healthy— Taft was also Chief Justice of the Supreme Court. Look it up."

"But he wasn't President and Chief Justice at the same time."

"Details! If he could be both, than so could I. I've already got this President thing down. What's so hard about being a justice? You just say 'Yea' or 'Nay' to stuff. I did that all the time on The Apprentice. Highest rated television show on NBC at the time. I doubt anyone's beat it."

"You may have a Republican majority in the House and Senate, but you can't just expect Congress to rubber stamp everything you do. This would be a bridge too far. Nominating yourself would just needlessly antagonistic— Are you listening?"

Donald J. Trump @realDonaldTrump
Congress if full of LOSERS. Also CRYBABIES. Congress cries itself to sleep at night. Sad.

"Mmm-mmmm" Trump said, tapping his phone.

The Vice President continued. "It's the nature of politics. Presidents don't always get everything they want."

Donal Trump's thumbs froze mid-tweet. His eyes inched up from his phone and landed coldly on the Vice President. "That's nonsense. That's impossible! I'm THE President. The people voted me in by a spectacular margin, the greatest margin ever in history. I have an entire holiday all to myself. Congress has to do what I say. That is what it says in the Constitution."

Mike Pence had already made good his retreat and was halfway out the door. "Good luck with that. Happy Presidents Day. I'll see you Tuesday."

Trump harrumphed a reply and returned to his phone.

 Donald J. Trump @realDonaldTrump
What's this country coming to if you can't nominate yourself to the Suprem Court? DRAIN THE SWAMP!

President Trump beamed at his perfectly sculpted tweet. It perfectly encapsulated every nuance of thought he had on the subject. It was so perfect, in fact, that he needed to show it off. He jumped from his chair and ventured into the halls of the White House. No one was around, the lights dim, the halls quiet. Melania had gone to New York, as she often did, with their son Barron. Most of the staff had taken off for the long weekend. And most everyone else had probably gone home, considering it was late on a Sunday afternoon and snow had begun piling up on the roads. Eventually, Donald found a lone intern, name unimportant.

"Intern, take a look at this," the President said, holding out his phone for inspection.

"I really wish you'd stop tweeting," the exasperated intern said, "and how many times do I have to tell you? I'm not an intern. I'm Reince Priebus, your White House Chief of Staff."

"My what now?"

"I used to be the Chair of the Republican National Committee," the completely unremarkable man said. "I'm very important to you having the support of the Republican Party during your election. That's why you gave me this position."

"Doesn't ring a bell."

"I've had you over to my house for dinner multiple times," the clearly pathetic and delusional intern said.

"Oh, dinner sounds fantastic," Donald Trump said, "Why don't you get me dinner?"

"That's not my job as White House Chief of Staff," the insubordinate intern said.

"You wouldn't want me to fire you and throw you away like a used Kleenex, would you? Because I could do that. White House Chief of Staff or not."

Sullen-faced, the intern accepted his fate as he had many times before, "The usual, then?"

"You got it."

Reince Priebus slunk away.

Donald J. Trump @realDonaldTrump
They don't make interns like they used to, right @BillClinton?

New Jersey Governor Chris Christie was standing in the Oval Office, measuring tape in hand, sizing the President's chair. "I'll have to bring in my own later," he mumbled to himself.

Trump's mood immediately soured. "What are you doing here, cream puff?"

"I heard that there's an opening on the Supreme Court," Christie said rubbing his doughy hands together.

"Nuh-uh." Trump waved his hand dismissively.

"Come on! I was the first Republican candidate to back you for President. I have experience as a United States Attorney." Chris Christie counted off on sausage-sized fingers and spoke through his teeth. "I also stood behind you during all those campaign rallies. I endured the shame. Even Jimmy Fallon making fun of me on the Tonight Show for it. Jimmy Fallon! I wish he'd just go back to telling fat jokes about me."

"That's why it can't be you, Chris," Donald Trump said, his The Apprentice persona shining through, "You did everything I wanted. You endured humiliation and ridicule. So much ridicule. Only a loser does that, and I can't have a loser on my Supreme Court." Trump raised his eyebrows and spread out his hands with a shrug of the shoulders.

Christie opened his mouth, about to raise another objection, but caught himself. He paused and then deliberately closed his mouth. Without another word he left the Oval Office.

 Donald J. Trump @realDonaldTrump
Who wants to see chris Christie do the truffle shuffle at my next rally? I guaranteE to make it happen.

Sitting on a chair right outside the Oval Office lay the President's usual dinner.

"At least the intern can do one thing right," Donald Trump said to himself. He picked up the grease-stained brown paper bag painted in golden arches and returned to his desk. Carefully opening the cardboard box, he revealed the quarter-pounder with cheese within. With erudite precision, he meticulously poured the contents of the fry box into the empty side of the burger box. Inside one of the drawers of his desk was a silver fork and knife which he used to carve his sandwich into small bites. He silently watched YouTube videos on his phone as he ate alone in the cavernous office.

With his meal done, he sat back in his chair, and drifted off to sleep.

2

"Donald Trump awoke at the sound of dragging footsteps, and low and bitter wailing, now far off, but growing closer. All the lights were out, and it was deathly cold. Moonlight reflected off the perfect blanket of snow covering the South Lawn, giving President Trump just enough light to see his own breath. He shivered and wondered who had turned off the lights and the thermostat. Trump glanced at his phone. It read "12:00am."

The moaning grew more distinct and nearer still. "Trump," it called just on the other side of the double doors to the Oval Office.

Frightened and alone, awoken in the middle of the night, a madman murmuring his name on the other side of a door, not knowing if this moment would be his last in this mortal coil, Donald Trump did what any other person would do in his situation. He picked up his phone and tweeted.

Donald J. Trump @realDonaldTrump
This is not a drill. All true Americans must
now come to my aide as is required in the
Constitution. Where is the Secret Service
when you ne

Donald J. Trump @realDonaldTrump
ed them?

"Trump," it called out again, emphatic.

Jumping to his feet, the President of the United States rushed across the Oval Office. Jittery hands fumbled with the door locks but found their target. Deadbolts latched with a heavy *CLACK*.

Trump took a few steps back from the door, and then called out, "No one's here," for good measure.

Then a most spectacular thing happened. Without opening, a figure stepped through the closed door. It was dressed in the regalia of an American general from the eighteenth century, but wrapped about him were ropes and cords and chains. They encircled him and tied around him in every direction, and they strung out behind him taut as if attached to some great weight. The cords and chains disappeared into the still closed door, the object they dragged still somewhere beyond the closed doors. He was tall, gaunt, and possessed a face Donald Trump knew well. It was the face emblazoned upon every twenty dollar bill. He was transparent and glowed an eerie shade of green reminiscent of US currency.

"Donald Trump," the apparition said.

"What's the meaning of this? Are you pulling some kind of prank? Who are you?" Trump said.

"Ask me who I was."

"What kind of question is that?"

"In life, I was the seventh President of the United States, Andrew Jackson."

Donald Trump glowered at the presence before him.

"You don't believe in me," said the ghost.

"Fake news," said Trump.

"Why do you doubt your senses?"

"Because you can't trust them," said Trump. "Everything's a fake nowadays. You could be a hologram made by the Chinese. They are a very clever people. Ruthless. Cunning."

The phantom stood there, silent, with a penetrating stare.

Donald Trump fished for another explanation. "Or, or, you're a hallucination, a very fake and very silly hallucination, brought on by—" he scanned his office, "—food poisoning! I just ate McDonalds. Who knows what they put into that stuff. I've seen *Super Size Me*, okay? They're cutting corners, padding their beef with magic mushrooms or some nonsense. You're just an undigested bit of beef. You're a blob of cheese. You're more special sauce than specter, that's for sure!"

Trump smiled at the joke he believed he had made.

The sudden urge to tweet it welled up inside him, but he couldn't decide how to give enough context in the space of 140 characters. He was about to attempt it anyway when the spirit unhinged its jaw and shrieked. It lunged forward and grabbed Trump by the lapels.

"Look into my eyes, Donald John Trump," it said, its breath as simultaneously freezing cold as it was blazing hot. Trump could do nothing but look into the creature's eyes. As he did, he realized he could also make out the back of Jackson's eyeballs, his skull, his brain, the hair on the back of his head. It was a gruesome and sickening sight. "Observe the bullet lodged near my heart," the ghost said, and Trump's gaze drifted downward. To his amazement he could see inside the ghost's chest. Wedged next to a heart that did not beat was a glinting metal fragment. "I received that wound in a duel in the year 1806. It remained there my entire life. Do you believe in me now?"

"Sure. Sure," Trump said, releasing himself from the ghost's grasp. "So why are you here? And make it snappy. I need to give some Hollywood losers a reality check. On Twitter."

 Donald J. Trump @realDonaldTrump
False alarm. Turned out to be the ghost of Pres Jackson.

"I have come to warn you, Trump. Heed my warning and avoid the fate that I made for myself."

Donald J. Trump @realDonaldTrump
And let me tell you something. Jackson sure is preachy for a dead guy.

"What are you doing with that infernal box? Are you listening to me?" Andrew Jackson's ghost said.

"Yeah, whatever," Trump said.

"You have been endowed with a grave responsibility that only forty-three men before you have possessed, Donald Trump. You should not take such things lightly. I, too, was a populist, elected by people in desire of change. But in my haste to carry out what my electors wanted from me, I hurt others. Countless thousands were dispossessed from their lands—Choctaw and Cherokee, Seminole and Creek. In life my electors praised me. Now in death I am cursed to bear the burden of each and every soul *I* burdened by my actions. I am destined to walk each ponderous, excruciating step I forced others to take whilst I was alive. This is my punishment; this is my penance."

"What does that have to do with me?" Trump huffed.

"It is a ponderous chain you are forging for yourself, Donald Trump. Your duty is not only to those who elected you, but to all mankind. It is not enough to be kind to only those who can benefit you. It is not enough to carry out the will of a few, while placing a weight on others. This is what I wish I had given thought to while I was yet alive. To be President is to be President of all. It is a glorious responsibility and affliction. What you require of people in this life will be required of you in the next."

"So, what? You came here to tell me to be a good President? Sorry you wasted a trip, bud, because I'm already the greatest President. I even have my own holiday."

"You will be haunted," said the ghost, "by Three Presidents."

"Like I said, I'm very busy—"

"Without their visits," continued the ghost, "you cannot hope to shun the path I tread. Expect the first when the phone tolls One."

"Couldn't I just take them all at once, and get it over with?"

"Expect the second at Two, and the third when the phone tolls Three. I must take my leave. My penance calls, and I still have many miles to tread."

With that said, President Jackson turned about and exited in the manner he came. His parting words were "Happy Presidents Day." As he stepped into the door, the heater activated with a click and a whir, and the lights in the Oval Office switched on. Donald Trump raced over to the doors and flung them open, but he saw nothing except dark, empty hallways.

 Donald J. Trump @realDonaldTrump
Jackson turned out to be a complete wimp. I couldve probably taken him.

Donald J. Trump @realDonaldTrump
Bad news, though. I gotta see three more of these losers before the night is done.

Trump sat in his chair behind the Resolute Desk. He contemplated the night's events before dismissing them entirely and falling into a quick slumber.

ERIC M. HAMILTON

3

"Wake up. It's morning in America!" a voice said, soothing as warm honey.

"Where am I? What time is it?" Donald Trump said as he shot awake.

"It's time for your rendezvous with destiny, Mr. Trump. I am the President of Presidents Day Past."

The form standing in front of Trump focused into view, it was a tall wrinkled man with perfectly combed dark brown hair and a dark navy suit, smartly pressed.

"Ronald Reagan," Donald Trump said, "So is this your past?"

"Yours. But also mine," Reagan said.

"So what are you here for?" Trump asked.

"Why don't we call it welfare reform?" Reagan said with a wink.

Donald J. Trump @realDonaldTrump
Second ghost, and already Reagan's
cracking jokes. Kill me now!

"Come with me," Reagan said, holding out his hand.

"Where are we going? Is it far?"

"Where we're going, we don't need roads."

In a flash, at the touch of Ronald Reagan's hand, Trump was standing in a room he had not been in for a long time. Two parallel lines of crisply made bunk beds marshaled a lengthy room. It was empty except for one blond boy in military dress, resting on one of the bottom bunks reading *MAD* magazine and chewing bubble gum. The boy was familiar to Trump for it was himself, though but a teenager.

"These are but shadows of the things that have been," the ghost of Ronald Reagan said. "The people here can neither see nor interact with us."

"This is Rosier Military Boarding School, and that's me," an astonished Trump said. "As good looking as ever."

"It is the year 1963. Your senior and final year at this academy," Reagan said.

"My parents sent me to hone my leadership qualities," Trump said.

"That's not how I understand it," Reagan said. "Rather, they needed discipline instilled in a young boy who snuck out with delinquent friends to Manhattan and bought a switch knife and hung out with hobos."

Before Trump could rebut the former President, an older man in full army regalia bounded into the room and stood at the foot of the bed that teenage Trump sat in. "A-TEEEEEEN-SION! Cadet Trump! What is the meaning of this?"

The young Donald Trump didn't even look up from his magazine. "What's up, Dobey?"

"Major Theodore Dobias," Reagan said, "a no-nonsense World War II veteran, and school administrator."

"I know who he is," the current President Trump said.

"What is the meaning of this," Dobias said, unconcerned and unaware of the ghostly conversation going on next to him.

"I'm taking a well-deserved rest," said Young Don.

"You were appointed Company Captain, and you're supposed to be inspecting the younger recruits' quarters."

"Yeah, I've got men on it," Young Don said, flipping a page of his magazine. "Promised Brown and O'Keefe five dollars each to do it for me. I can't be bothered with the small stuff. Once I'm out of here, my father has a small one million dollar 'loan' waiting for me to start my business."

Donald J. Trump @realDonaldTrump
I was clever when I was young. I really
should appoint MYSELF to the Supreme
Court.

Donald J. Trump @realDonaldTrump
Also had great hair. THE GREATEST. Still do

Major Dobias let out an audible sigh, "You can't just pay people to do your work for you."

Young Don looked up from his magazine, confused, "But I did."

"It's clear to me that you cannot handle the responsibilities that come with being Company Captain. You're being reassigned to the school administration office."

Young Don lit up, "A promotion!"

"No, it's so I can keep an eye on you," Major Dobias asserted.

"Oh, you need me close. I'm too valuable to be babysitting new recruits."

Dobias sighed again, "Sure."

"You've always had a problem with authority," Ronald Reagan observed. "Your parents tried to help you, your teachers tried to help you, but you just did whatever you felt like doing. You were like a baby, a big appetite at one end, and no sense of responsibility at the other."

President Trump sneered, "Did we just watch the same thing? I delegated authority and got promoted to my true potential. Besides, no one was hurt."

"Let us go to another time, then," said Reagan. "Take my hand."

At the touch of the ghost's hand, Trump was transported to Fifth Avenue in New York City. It was the middle of the day; the sun was bright and warm. People bustled to and fro down the busy sidewalk.

"These people, too, have no consciousness of us," said the specter. "Though I guess that wouldn't really matter since it's New York in 1983. It's the era of greed, the "me decade" as some called it. But I don't have to remind you."

Out of the corner of Donald Trump's eye, he caught sight of something quite unforgettable—himself. He was in his thirties, and he was getting out of a limousine. It was all coming back to him, the real estate deals, the rough and tumble day-to-day business of building a fortune. If there was any time that he truly felt alive it was this. Trump watched his incredibly handsome doppelganger rush across the sidewalk, right in front of him. Donald attempted to get his own attention, but his younger self continued into the building without a glance. Donald turned to watch his younger self enter the recently christened Trump Tower.

Donald J. Trump @realDonaldTrump
Fantastic does not begin to describe me at my prime. But it's a start.

Donald J. Trump @realDonaldTrump
I am one of the few people to have been in their prime their entire lives. Absolutely true

"Like I said," Reagan repeated, "they can't see or hear us. This is what's already happened."

"Why are you showing me this?" Trump asked.

"To remind you. You made your fortune in real estate, while I was in office. In some ways, you could say the Trump legacy started here. It was the decade of greed, some say, and others lay the praise or the blame directly at my feet. Following the Carter recession, it was mostly inevitable, though. As President, there is only so much that you can actually do to alter the course of things. And even the things you try to alter don't always have their intended effects."

"The eighties were good to me," Trump said.

"And yet you were a Democrat then. It's okay, I don't hold it against you. I used to be one, too." Reagan chuckled. "You know, as a President, you can't get everything perfect. Even the most carefully considered choices tragically leave some unfortunate souls worse off. I was not perfect. No man is. I don't want you to think this whole exercise is to tell you to reach an unattainable standard of perfection. It's not possible.

Yet, you have to know every decision comes with a cost. You knew that when you bought and sold real estate, once upon a time."

Reagan was almost wistful as he watched the random people passing by in front of them, off to their individual destinations, unaware of the spectral Presidents that stood amid them.

"One of the most important things to realize is that it really is not about you at all. It's about the American people you serve. Just like any other people, they will return what you give them. If you fill them with hope, and desire, and a belief that tomorrow will be better than yesterday, they will surprise you like you've never been surprised. If, instead, you fill them with fear, and hatred, and a belief that what they had yesterday may be lost tomorrow, well, I'm certain they will surprise you in that case as well."

Donald J. Trump @realDonaldTrump
Reagan brought me back to New York City, 1983. The people can't see or hear me. I've got one word: RUDE.

"I have one more thing to show you," the ghost of Ronald Reagan said, holding out his hand.

This time the two men were instantly transported to Moscow, standing in the Red Square in front of the Kremlin. Again, there was a large crowd of people, but not scurrying about in all directions as people were in New York City. Instead, they all gathered around one figure. Reagan led Trump over, navigating through the crowds, until Trump could finally see who was the center of attention. It was President Reagan.

Ghost Reagan did not seem interested in his living counterpart though. Instead, he guided Trump over to a young man in the crowd, standing to the side, carefully watching the American President's every move. He had smartly combed blond hair and a striped shirt. Binoculars hung around his neck.

"You certainly know this man," the ghost said, "at this time, KGB operative. But presently—"

"Russian President Vladimir Putin," Donald Trump breathed.

"We all have pasts that inform our present," Reagan said. "Perhaps you should not only recall your past, but his as well. Don't get me wrong. I'm all for diplomacy. Trust, but verify."

"Okay, I get it. Scary commie guy. Can't trust him. Whatever. I can handle him. Are we done yet?" Trump said.

"Many a man has failed because he had a wishbone where his backbone should have been," the former President said.

"What is that even supposed to mean? I'm done with riddles! Done!" Trump shouted. In the blink of an eye, he was again in the White House. Alone.

Donald J. Trump @realDonaldTrump
How many times do I have to say this about President Reagan? OVER RATED.

Donald J. Trump @realDonaldTrump
But Putin—now there's a CLASSY guy. Great dresser too!

ERIC M. HAMILTON

4

This time, Trump determined to stay awake through the two o'clock hour. He refused to be awoken by a third spirit in same night. He watched his phone tick away the minutes on the digital display. As it hit "2:00am" Trump expected some ghost to pop out of nowhere, but no specter was to be seen.

 Donald J. Trump @realDonaldTrump
Ghosts must have given up. I think I proved to them how great a President I am.

From somewhere else in the White House, Trump could hear music playing. Trump waited a moment, listening, but as the music continued, he decided he needed to investigate. He left the Oval Office and followed the sound of the music. It was orchestral but tinny, as if played through an ancient speaker. It brought him to the first floor East Room. Light shone through underneath the closed doors. In addition to the music, Trump could hear laughter, a loud and full belly laugh, coming from the room typically used for balls and other state functions.

Donald Trump hesitated in front of the doors, wondering what intruder may have broken into the White House. He was about to turn back when a voice from inside the East Room bellowed out.

"Well, come in, man! Don't leave me waiting here all night!"

Trump opened the doors, and bright lights spilled into the dark and dreary hall. The strong and distinct waft of wonderful food hit Trump at the same time as the light.

"Come in. Come in and know me better, man," the voice said.

Trump stepped into the East Room, and his eyes refocused to an astonishing sight. The entire ballroom was filled to the brim with the stuffed remains of almost every type of game on earth: Deer, elk, bears, moose, lions, tigers, elephants, and many more. It was almost like stepping into Noah's Ark, if Noah had been a taxidermist. At the center of the room a large table was stocked with the most delectable looking foods, and sitting at the table was a man dressed in khaki-colored hunting attire. Atop his head rested a cowboy hat with one side pinned up. He had circular glasses and a discernible gap between his two front teeth, which he bore in a gigantic smile beneath a glorious mustache.

"Bully!" he declared. "I'm the President of Presidents Day Present! Ha! Say that five times fast!"

Donald J. Trump @realDonaldTrump
Someone tell safari man here that its presidents day. Not Halloween

"And you are?" Trump said.

"You—you haven't seen me before?" the ghost's mustache wilted a bit.

"You look familiar."

"Theodore Roosevelt. Youngest man to become President."

"An overachiever?"

"I helped end the Russo-Japanese War. I received a Nobel Peace Prize for my efforts."

"Nobel Prize is a scam."

"My visage is set upon Mount Rushmore."

"Not ringing a bell. Wait. Washington, Jefferson, Lincoln, and—Oh! You're the *other* one."

Roosevelt pursed his lips in frustration. "Quite." He quickly regained his cheerful composure, however, as if he had been nothing but.

Donald J. Trump @realDonaldTrump
Gottem! Had to bring Teddy down a peg. Too cheerful. It's creepy, creepier than being a ghost

"When I was selected as President McKinley's Vice President," the former President said, "it was not meant as the honor some would think. I had many adversaries in the Republican Party, and they had given me a job with hardly any power whatsoever. They thought they could neuter my popular appeal by denying me the presidency. Many in my party saw me as dangerous, uncontrollable, and unpredictable."

Trump tilted his head in a shrug. "Sounds familiar."

"And to give them credit, I may have been. I can only admit that now in my after-life. I never would have then. Truth be told, I was wild and dangerous. It had been perfectly fine for me to take risks with my own life and fortune. But there's something about the presidency. It changes a man, or at least it ought to change a man. It's no longer just yourself you must consider. And you not only have a responsibility to the citizens living now, but to countless unborn generations blessed enough to call the United States their home. You have a responsibility to posterity everlasting. You must leave the country better than it was delivered unto you."

Donald J. Trump @realDonaldTrump
Should I grow a mustache? I can't stop staring at this guy's mustache.

Roosevelt sniffed his nose, "Well, we have much to see, and not much time to see it. It is the present, and only so much of it until it passes us by, never to return."

Instantaneously, Roosevelt and Trump were transported to a snow-covered Irving Street on the north side of Washington, D.C. They stood beneath red glowing letters spelling out "IHOP RESTAURANT."

"Why have you brought me here, Spirit?" Trump asked.

"Inside this International House of Pancakes sits a man, lonely and dejected. His Presidents Day is not going as well as he hoped for. Take a look." Roosevelt beckoned Trump to peer through the window into the 24-hour establishment. "Don't worry, he can't see you."

Trump wiped his sleeve over the frosted glass, until he made for himself a porthole through which he could see. Inside, squeezed into a booth, was the Governor of New Jersey. He had barely touching his stack of buttermilk pancakes topped in an obscene amount of syrup. Trump audibly groaned.

"Keep watching," Roosevelt chided.

A few seconds later, White House intern Reince Priebus joined the Governor, sitting in the seat opposite him. "Hi, Chris," he said. "It was a no go, huh?"

Chris Christie shook his head. "You know, I really thought I had made the right move in the primaries. Trump was a long shot, but I was the first to endorse him before anyone else did. Look where it got me."

"This path he's on. He treats his enemies harshly, and his allies harsher," Reince said. "I thought this was going to be a stepping stone, you know? Work in the

White House, make some political connections, run for governor or senator or something, but it's all about him. It's all about Trump. When is it ever going to be about Priebus?"

Donald J. Trump @realDonaldTrump
Whoever runs against the Tiny Intern, let me know. You have my endorsement

"I think I might just need to resign, get out of politics," Priebus continued. "Maybe get into real estate or insurance or something. I'm just not cut out for this."

"Oh no!" Trump gasped. "Spirit, my intern might leave me? What will happen to Tiny Intern?"

"I am only allowed to see the present, but I see in the corner a boring desk job, and a broken dream."

"No, I meant who is going to get me my Big Macs when I get hungry? He's a lousy intern, but at least he gets my order correct."

As Trump fretted over the impending shake up in his dinner routine, Vice President Mike Pence entered the establishment and sat in the booth with the two men. "Happy Presidents Day, gentlemen," he said.

Governor Christie snorted, "A fine 'happy' one it is, too."

"Just another day to celebrate an insufferable wretch of a man," Priebus added.

"Gentlemen," Pence said, "Our President is indeed the most loathsome of creatures. Greedy, arrogant, corrupt, unintelligent, and the most undeserving man to have ever been given the title President of the United States—"

"Traitors everywhere I look!" Trump exclaimed.

Donald J. Trump @realDonaldTrump
This ghost thing, not being able to be seen, is pretty useful. spying on my enemies. Very bad people. #DrainTheSwamp

"Keep listening," Roosevelt said, "there is still more."

Mike Pence continued, "—yet he is the President. And the office still has some dignity left to it. And our political positions are kept alive thanks to him. We all could—" Pence paused, eyes shifting uncomfortably, and began again, "—two of us could one day be President ourselves. It's important we don't allow the office to become so damaged that we cannot occupy it later. Like it or not, we have to play the long game. Politics properly played is the long game."

The Governor and the intern nodded at the Vice President's words.

"Like I said. Traitors!" Trump said as he typed furiously at his phone.

Donald J. Trump @realDonaldTrump
Reminder: Don't trust Pence with anything.

Donald J. Trump @realDonaldTrump
On 2d thought, I don't need a reminder.
I've got one fantastic memory.

"They aren't traitors so much as individuals with their own lives and political agendas," Theodore Roosevelt said. "These men could be your allies, but they aren't just going to do something because you are President and they are not. A President cannot accomplish anything without understanding the motivations of others beneath him. The game of politics should not be about winners and losers, but in advancing justice and peace for all people."

"Politics is about getting things done. And winners get things done."

Theodore Roosevelt sighed, "Well, you can bring a horse to water, but you can't make him drink."

"Who are you calling horse-faced?"

"Unfortunately, my time grows short," Roosevelt said, the IHOP and the ghost fading into darkness. "Hopefully he will sort you out."

"What? Who will sort me out?" Trump said, but he was already back in the White House in an unlit and empty East Room.

5

The phone read "3:00am," and Trump was still dreading the appearance of him. He sat erect at his desk, waiting for the third ghost to appear. One moment the room was empty, the next, in the blink of an eye, a man stood before him. He was unremarkable in his appearance, completely forgettable, just another man one might pass in the street. He was dressed handsomely but old-fashioned. His face bore no expression, neither positive nor negative. He simply stood before President Trump and looked at him, eye-to-eye.

"Am I in the presence of the President of Presidents Day Yet to Come?" said Trump.

The Spirit did not answer. He just stood.

"Ha. Say that five times fast." Trump's voice faltered into an uncharacteristic whisper. The imposing specter shook Trump's being in a way he rarely felt.

The man raised his hand and pointed onward.

"You're about to show me shadows of the things that have not yet happened, but will happen. Is that right?"

The man slightly inclined his head and continued to point.

Donald J. Trump @realDonaldTrump
This last ghost needs to clean out his ears!
Total. Loser.

"President of the Future," Trump said, "I am confident that the future only shows great things, the greatest things. I am prepared for what you will show me. Lead on!"

The figure pointed once more, and Trump turned in the direction the apparition indicated. As he turned, he found himself no longer in the White House, but on a busy street sidewalk in a major city. People were going about their day, working, shopping, chatting. Everyone seemed to be in a cheerful and pleasant mood, and somewhere in the distance, Trump could hear birds singing.

"Good day to be alive, isn't it? And a good day to be proud to be an American, I'd say!" said one person to another.

"It certainly is!" the other responded. "Things are looking up with our President! He's certainly turned things around! I can't think of a time other than right this moment when there was no internal strife within the country at all and everyone genuinely gets along."

"Haha! Ain't that the truth?"

Trump turned about on the silent specter. "See, I told you! The future is fantastic! Clearly, I was a fantastic President! I fixed everything. Didn't you hear them praising the President? Me!"

The ghost turned and pointed toward what appeared to be a television screen, except that it was paper thin and set flush with the exterior wall of a storefront building. On the screen was a news reporter.

"—and here is a portion of what President Chris Christie said earlier today at the El Paso-Juarez border with Mexico."

The feed cut to an elderly Chris Christie, perhaps in his seventies and rather quite svelte, speaking to a gathered crowd. "Today, we celebrate the continuing partnership we enjoy with our neighbors to the south. There is no greater bond than that of the people of Mexico and the United States."

 Donald J. Trump @realDonaldTrump
That traitor Christie looked better when he was fat. JUST SAYING!

Trump turned away from the screen. "Okay, this is considerably farther in the future than I thought. But Christie is just benefiting from my policies. My big, beautiful wall (that Mexico paid for). Spirit, take me to the Mexican border!"

With a sweeping gesture, the ghost waved his hand

and suddenly the two were standing in a wide open space, desert in all directions. No man-made structures at all.

"No, Spirit. I told you to take me to the Mexican border. This can't be the border, because my wall isn't here."

The spirit continued to say nothing, but pointed once again. Trump turned to see a small plaque sitting by itself in the barren wasteland. Trump cautiously approached it, and as he came nearer, he could read what it said: "WELCOME TO MEXICO." And below that: "BIENVENIDOS A MEXICO." Trump then ran to the opposite side of the sign and read, "WELCOME TO THE UNITED STATES. BIENVENIDO A LOS ESTADOS UNIDOS."

"No. It can't be! Spirit! What does this mean?"

Finally, the spirit spoke. "My name is Millard Fillmore."

Trump was thoroughly confused. "What? I thought all of you guys were supposed to be Presidents. Are you actually a President from the future where old-timey things come back into fashion?"

"I was the thirteenth President of the United States. I served from 1850 to 1853," the ghost said.

"How can that be? I've never heard of a Millard Fillmore. What are you remembered for?"

"Nothing."

"That doesn't make any sense," Trump said. "Presidents are always remembered for something. They're *Presidents*!"

With another sweep of the hand, Millard Fillmore

brought Donald Trump into a sixth-grade classroom studying history.

"Okay, class, who can tell me the Presidents of the early 21st century?" the teacher said.

The nerdy kid without any friends frantically waved his hand.

"Go ahead, Donald."

"Well, technically Bill Clinton was President in January of 2000," he said.

The teacher rolled her eyes, "Yes, technically correct, Donald. Who came next?"

"Then was George W. Bush, and Barack Obama, and Joe Biden, and then, uhm Alexandria Ocasio-Cortez, and—"

"No, Alexandria Ocasio-Cortez is the Chief Justice of the Supreme Court."

"Oh, yeah."

"You're forgetting the one in between Barack Obama and Joe Biden, Donald."

"I am? I memorized them all last night. Who am I missing?"

Trump was reeling. "It's literally *your name*, you silly child!" he pleaded.

"They can't hear you," Fillmore reminded Trump.

The teacher furrowed her brow. "You know what? I don't remember, either. I'm going to have to look it up."

Donald Trump convulsed with pain.

"Here it is," she said. "Donald Tr-Tremp? There's a smudge on this page. That must be it. Donald Tremp."

The entire classroom of children could not have

been less interested.

Donald was on his hands and knees, about to puke. "Show me no more, Spirit. I beg of you. I cannot bear it."

The spirit of Millard Fillmore left Donald Trump, and the President of the United States was left huddled, alone, in the Oval Office.

Now it's time to choose your own ending! How will this night of ghoulish visitation affect the President of the United States? It's up to you!

If you think Donald Trump is a horrible human being and a horrible President—

He does not, indeed he cannot, learn any lesson. Positive change is beyond his grasp, and frankly, he shouldn't get the opportunity to repent. Trump deserves what's coming to him. And in all honesty, the author should be canceled for the audacity to write a book featuring such a despicable man. **TURN TO PAGE 85**.

If you think Donald Trump has nothing to learn—

Sure, he says some rude things now and again, but you need a straight talker and a straight shooter to bring change to a corrupt federal government and drain the swamp. This whole book has just been one cheap liberal political attack against our greatest President to ever have lived. **TURN TO PAGE 95**.

If you have a neutral opinion about Donald Trump—

You do not exist. It is literally impossible for you to not have one of the two previous opinions about Trump. So stop lying to yourself and to the rest of us, and go back and select one of the other two links.

ERIC M. HAMILTON

You may have not noticed, but you were supposed to select one of the choices.
Please turn back a page and select an ending.

ERIC M. HAMILTON

You're still turning the page forward.
This is not how this works.
TURN TO PAGE 41 to go back to the choice.

ERIC M. HAMILTON

Are you even reading any of this?
This is not the best way to enjoy this book.
Turn back and choose an ending.

ERIC M. HAMILTON

For maximum enjoyment, I beg of you,
please go back and make a choice.

ERIC M. HAMILTON

What do you think you're accomplishing by stubbornly turning the page?

So, it's going to be this way.
Me trying to convince you to pick an ending,
and you just turning pages like a lemming
bounding for the cliffside.

ERIC M. HAMILTON

I can't convince you, can I?

ERIC M. HAMILTON

Oops, you forgot something very important.
TURN TO PAGE 41 to return to a
VERY IMPORTANT thing that you're missing.
Super important. Trust me.

ERIC M. HAMILTON

Still going, huh?

Fine.
Have it your way.
The next page contains a
SUPER SECRET ending just for you.
Enjoy.

ERIC M. HAMILTON

?

"Ante up." The baritone voice boomed, gruff and direct.

Donald Trump had once again fallen asleep at his desk. He opened his eyes to find a man sitting opposite him at the other side of the Resolute Desk. A single light shining from high above illuminated the desk and left the rest of the Oval Office in a dark, infinite void.

"Well?" the man said. He had neatly combed white hair, thick black eyebrows, and the wrinkles of his face set an unmovable scowl that seemed to be chiseled from stone rather than flesh. His eyes were cast down on his own hand of five cards. "Are you even going to look at your cards?"

Trump looked down in front of him to find five playing cards face down, as well as his cell phone which read "4:00am." He found the Resolute Desk to have also changed; a green felt cloth covered its surface. Trump picked up his phone instead of the cards.

Donald J. Trump @realDonaldTrump
These losers just won't stop showing up!

Without lifting his cards, Trump stared the latest specter in his cold, dead eyes. "There were only supposed to be three of you," he said, folding his hands together. "I was done. Finished. I don't want to deal with more of you losers than I have to."

"Patience, Donald Trump," the stone-faced man said, eyes still focused on his hand, and then with the hint of a smile that was still mostly scowl, "Jackson can be a bit dramatic. He always was. Reagan and Roosevelt, too much dazzled by their lofty ideals even in death. And Fillmore has yet to recover from the resentment of being utterly forgotten. But I am here to give a, shall we say, dissenting opinion."

"Yeah? And what're you going to say that I haven't heard already?"

The man with the thick eyebrows lifted his eyes and stared straight back into Donald Trump's. Unblinking, he said, "I am Warren Harding. I was President of the United States during a time of unparalleled peace and prosperity." Harding paused a moment but did not waver from his stare. "Yet, no one now knows me, and it is a blessing."

Donald J. Trump @realDonaldTrump
All of these ghosts just trying to cope with they're failure

Donald J. Trump @realDonaldTrump
If I ever do this as a ghost KILL ME

Trump met and returned Harding's gaze. "I don't believe you. If you were so great, why haven't I heard of you? And if you were so great, why are you happy to be forgotten?"

Harding's eyes fell to his cards. "There are some things we'd rather not be known, like in poker. The advantage lies just as much with what is hidden as with what is known."

Trump continued to stare.

"Well, are you going to play?" Warren Harding motioned to the cards still face down in front of the President.

"What are the stakes? I never play without knowing the stakes."

"Indiscretions, gaffes, misjudgments, sins," the ghost of Warren Harding listed. "Anything you would rather be forgotten by posterity."

Donald Trump leaned back in his seat. "I don't have any of those."

Harding returned his glare to Trump. "Nothing?"

Trump shrugged, eyebrows lifted in befuddlement.

Warren Harding's lips pursed ever so slightly. "Then we shall play for your time."

This caught Donald Trump's attention. He sat up straighter. "If I win, you'll leave me alone?"

Harding nodded.

"Best news I've heard all night," the President said and promptly turned over his cards revealing three Kings and two Threes.

Warren Harding's left eyebrow twitched.

"Full house. That's a terrific hand if I say so myself. I win." Donald said as he folded his hands in satisfaction.

Harding regained his composure and placed his cards face down on the table. "No, I'm afraid not. Take a walk with me, Mr. President." Warren Harding stood.

 Donald J. Trump @realDonaldTrump
Ha! Called his bluff and he knows it.

"Show me your cards first," Trump said to the specter. "I am done with ghosts."

Harding's hard eyes bored into Trump's. "I once lost the White House china playing cards. I learned my lesson in life, never to make a bet I did not intend to win."

The former President flipped over his card revealing four Sixes and one Five. "I believe four of a kind *trumps* full house."

"You cheated! You never shuffled the deck. You gave me a losing hand."

Harding merely shrugged. "Need a recount?"

 Donald J. Trump @realDonaldTrump
Does anyone ever feel like dejavu but the first time?

"Can we make this quick? I'd rather be doing anything else. Quite literally anything else," Trump moaned as he got to his feet.

"We aren't going far," Harding said, "we're already here, in fact."

The light in the Oval Office grew, revealing the rest of the room, though still in the hazy gloom of twilight. As the light revealed the room, so too were dozens of figures illuminated, each about his own business. Some were very recognizable, others not so much, but they all had the distinct bearing of men given the highest office of leadership.

Warren Harding elaborated, "When you become President, you inherit a legacy of the past. This White House is a nexus for all the decisions made here that echo out into eternity. Whether occupied lengthily or briefly, each left their indelible mark. But some marks are left deeper than others."

Trump could see the ghosts of Presidents from the recent past all the way back to the nation's beginning. They all sputtered about aimlessly as ghosts do, imitating the actions they performed in life: Looking at papers, pacing about, napping while someone else did their job for them, presidential things.

"We're elected to perform a job, but it's not necessary." Harding motioned to one of the napping figures lying supine on a couch. The ghost had a long face and round glasses, his hands folded neatly on his chest. "My predecessor, Woodrow Wilson, suffered a stroke late into his second term, and his health declined so sharply that his wife essentially ran the country, controlling who could see him and making decisions in his name. The rumors at the time were fiercely denied. Now, it's accepted history." Warren Harding would have frowned if his face were not fixed in a permanent frown already. "It doesn't matter. No one cares that a President was mentally unable to perform his duty."

"But that was back in the Stone Ages without constant news coverage and cameras everywhere," Trump protested. "Surely a President couldn't get away with something like that now."

"What's up, Jack?" An oddly familiar voice said. The former Vice President, Joe Biden stood before Donald Trump. He wore aviators and held a dripping ice cream cone in one hand. He seemed corporeal and solid, unlike all the other ghosts which Trump could see through if he focused hard enough. "I am the Ghost of Christmas—no wait, that's not right. I'm the Ghost of the thing, you know."

"You're not dead, Joe," Donald Trump said. "You are many many horrible things, but dead is not one of them."

Joe Biden waved another wandering specter in old-timey clothing and a powdered wig over to them, "Hey, you there. This is the Father of our Constipation- no, that's our Coronation- no, our you know."

"James Madison," the ghost said, clearly annoyed, "Father of the Constitution."

"That's what I've been saying, the Mother of our Computer Station. Listen. Tell Donald the thing."

The ghost of James Madison sighed, "Since time has no meaning outside of a physical context, the spirits of the dead exist in a space beyond time. Our visages are mere echoes of the lives we lived. The echo can reverberate not only forward, but backward as well."

"Prezzactly," Joe Biden slurred. "I'm a backtrack echo thingie—ghost."

"So, you're the ghost of a guy who hasn't died yet."

"Exactomundo."

"Then does that mean you'll be President before you die?"

"What are you talking about? Barap Jemima is President. Anyway, I want to tell you to listen to this guy here." Biden motioned to Warren Harding. "Not only does he have a funny name, but he knows his *trunalimunumaprzure*. He just hasn't shared it with me. But I tell you what, I don't know about you, but I'm going to go to bed." Joe Biden then turned and shuffled off in a random direction and through a wall.

Donald J. Trump @realDonaldTrump
You better hope these are just visions of what may be rather than what will be, or WE ARE ALL IN TROUBLE

Donald J. Trump @realDonaldTrump
Just sayin.

Warren Harding was not fazed. "Political ambition covers a multitude of sins. The American people consider themselves a moral people, but they are willing to look over a number of things if they can achieve what they want politically."

"Oh, believe me. I know," Trump said.

The ghost of Harding walked over to another section of the Oval Office. Several men distinctly dressed from different eras of American history were sitting at a table engaged in a card game of their own. One was clearly inebriated, but winning, causing no small amount of consternation among the others.

"Yahoo! Royal flush! Read 'em and weep!" the ghost of Lyndon Baines Johnson whooped as the other men sighed in varying degrees of exasperation. "And I'm not talking about the royal flush I have to take every time I—"

"Please," said the ghost of Thomas Jefferson, "we've heard it all before."

"But have you seen it?" LBJ would not be

suppressed. "We should have a measuring contest to see which one of you would be in second place."

"President Johnson was known for being crass," Harding said.

"It's not crass if it's the truth," Johnson interjected.

"Speaking of truth," President Trump said, "is it true about Kennedy?"

"No one can prove that!" Johnson yelled. "And you better not release any of those classified files, or so help me, I will haunt you the rest of your life."

 Donald J. Trump @realDonaldTrump
Nothing is worth a lifetime of LBJ bragging about his covfefe

"Some sins are more overt," Warren Harding said. "Some of us had children out of wedlock. Jefferson's have come more to light in your time. Grover Cleveland had the mother of his illegitimate child sent to an asylum. Even I had a child with a mistress thirty-one years my junior."

"What's the point of telling me all of this?" Trump asked.

"Context," Harding said. "Sure, people care at the time, and they use such allegations, whether true or not, to take you out of the game. But it's nothing personal. It's just politics. You aren't special. You may make headlines, and hundreds of thousands of words may be written about your various misdeeds. But eventually, given enough time, you'll simply be a footnote, a statistic, and eventually nothing."

Warren Harding's lip trembled just a bit, and Trump thought he could see tears forming in his eyes for a moment. But Harding blinked and recomposed himself.

"And that is a good thing."

Well, are you happy you read that extra chapter? Good. Because you still have a choice to make. You can't avoid it forever.

-If you think Donald Trump is irredeemably evil and deserves to be thrown out of office,
TURN TO PAGE 85.

-If you think Donald Trump is the only thing keeping America from descending into lawless abandon,
TURN TO PAGE 95.

-Again, it is not humanly possible to not have one of those two opinions, so choose one of the two options above. Do not blindly turn the next page.

ERIC M. HAMILTON

So, we're going to do this again?

ERIC M. HAMILTON

Are you just incapable of making decisions,
or do you just refuse to follow directions?

ERIC M. HAMILTON

You must be a wonderful person to be around.

ERIC M. HAMILTON

That was sarcasm if you couldn't tell.
I'm sure you couldn't.
That's why I'm telling you.

ERIC M. HAMILTON

Might as well just keep turning the page.
Your indecision has brought you
to one of the two choices anyway.

ERIC M. HAMILTON

6α

Dawn broke, and light from the morning sun woke Donald Trump, who had been lying asleep on the floor of the Oval Office. He jumped up and inspected the name placard on his desk. It read "Donald J. Trump." He was still President!

He burst into the White House hallway, clicking his heels, celebrating his opportunity to set things right. Mike Pence, Chris Christie, and the intern happened to be walking down the hall and observed the bizarre spectacle.

 Donald J. Trump @realDonaldTrump
Oh no! Larry Moe and Curly. Gotta keep up appearances

Donald Trump regained his composure and straightened his suit. "Humph," growled Trump, in a gruff voice he could barely contain, "What tributes have you brought me for President's Day? You know it's President's Day, right? My day. My terrific day, all for me."

The three men looked at one another, and the intern spoke up. "Tribute?"

"I think, as President, I would know the traditional way to celebrate President's Day." Trump said. "Oh, and I think I'm going to appoint someone to the Supreme Court who follows and applies the law fairly. So fair you wouldn't believe it."

The three men stood slack-jawed and aghast.

"B-but what about me?" said Chris Christie.

"You can't do that!" the intern blurted out.

"Sure I can. It'll be fantastic. I can see the tweets now: *Greatest President appoints Greatest Justice*."

"It's happened. He's gone mad," said the intern, "absolutely bonkers."

"Why not someone from an approved Republican list?" Vice President Pence encouraged.

Trump kept talking as if he did not hear. "And then we better get cracking on that wall. Don't forget to make Mexico pay for it. Then we'll drop out of NATO, renegotiate our free trade agreements, and make fun of the ruler of North Korea on Twitter just for fun."

Pence muttered to the other two as Trump continued listing his completely unrealistic policies, "He has to be stopped."

Mike Pence was better than his word. Citing Trump's clear descent into madness, the Vice President invoked the 25th Amendment. By the end of the day, he obtained every Cabinet Secretary's signature, effectively removing the President from active duty and making Pence Acting President. The following morning, the Congress brought up impeachment charges against the President. All manner of impropriety and criminal mischief was uncovered: Collusion with the Russians, the Chinese, the Iranians, the Togolese, the Liechtensteiners, just to name a few. There were so many people willing to testify to being bribed and threatened and coerced by President Trump that the impeachment trial lasted over sixteen months with gavel-to-gavel coverage on all the major news networks. After such overwhelming evidence of high crimes and misdemeanors, the President was impeached by the House and removed from office by a unanimous vote of the Senate. Everyone remarked on the wonderful symbolism that such a historic event happened to coincide on July 4.

"Our long national nightmare is over," President Mike Pence declared in his televised remarks to the nation that evening. In his speech he declared that "that scoundrel" would be exiled to an uninhabited island in the Pacific. The entire nation was so elated for the salvation of democracy that no one quite understood the implications of Pence's promise to "bring sanctity back to the White House and the nation."

The next day, Pence signed a series of executive orders that collectively came to be known as the "Trump Reversal Acts" (TRAs). Anything that even had a hint of being Trumpian was banned from American life. Trump was known for plastering his name on buildings he owned, so signs of every kind were forbidden. Trump had an unusual hair style, and so hair styles were mandated based on, of course, Pence and the First Lady. Trump had a penchant for gold and silver, so all valuable metals, jewels, and gemstones were seized by the government for the public's good. Anyone who objected was swiftly jailed, and thanks to another one of the TRAs, they were not allowed to defend themselves, since speaking on behalf of oneself was arrogant and boastful, a very Trumpian thing to do.

More TRAs were passed as it became clear that other things in American life were just too Trumpish to be allowed to remain unchecked. Trump had only been President for a short time, so President Pence was given a lifetime term so he wouldn't be anything like Trump. Trump was known as a hedonist with many, many moral problems, and thus a strict moral code was enforced upon the nation. Since Trump was twice divorced, divorce for any reason was banned. Since Trump had extramarital affairs, premarital relations (even up to hand holding) was forbidden. Sometimes Donald Trump said bad words, and so curse words of any kind, including Trumpian curses like "losers" and "horse-faced" were forbidden. Trump said what was on his mind, and so having an unapproved opinion was nixed as well. Some brave souls tried to challenge these government actions in court, claiming they were violations of the Bill of Rights. The government's lawyers simply said, "But that's what Trump did," and the Supreme Court agreed that any act deemed

Trumpian was not protected by the Constitution.

The American people, all with their approved haircuts, approved dress, approved luxuries, approved speech, and approved thoughts, were thankful to have a President like Mike Pence. Indeed they had no other choice! It was always said of Pence that he knew how to keep America free from Trumpism well, if any man alive possessed the knowledge. May that be truly said of us, and all of us! At least we're not anything like Donald Trump!

THE END

Okay, maybe it would've been better if Trump was just left alone. **TURN TO PAGE 95** *to see how that turns out.*

ERIC M. HAMILTON

You should not have ever gotten to this page unless you're just going through every page in order. That's not the point of choosing your own ending.

ERIC M. HAMILTON

Well, it doesn't matter much.
The other ending starts on the next page.
I guess your stubbornness paid off in the end.
Congratulations.

ERIC M. HAMILTON

6Ω

Dawn broke, and light from the morning sun woke Donald Trump, who had been lying asleep on the floor of the Oval Office. He jumped up and inspected the name placard on his desk. It read "Donald J. Trump." He was still President!

Outside, Trump spied a small boy, perhaps seven or eight, dragging a sled behind him in the freshly fallen snow. Trump threw open the windows of the Oval Office and yelled out to the boy.

"Hey, aren't you supposed to be in school?"

The boy called back, "But today is Presidents Day. There is no school."

"Presidents Day? I haven't missed it! The spirits did it all in one night. Well of course they can, they can do anything." Trump shouted back, "Boy, can you do one more thing for me?"

"Sure thing, Mister President."

"Get off my lawn! Where's the Secret Service when you need them? What am I paying them for?" Donald

Trump continued to grumble to himself as he closed the windows.

Trump was better than his word. He did it all and infinitely more. He began pushing all of his programs through Congress, and those he could not push through Congress, he ensured by Executive Order. He appointed judges in his likeness, filled positions in the government with his cronies. He built his southern border wall (and made Mexico pay for it), fought trade wars with China, abandoned allies in Europe over funding of NATO, and a myriad of other accomplishments too numerous to recount.

But as is the case with all things, Trump's power became ensconced. Ineffective policies were replaced with different ineffective policies. Shrewd bureaucrats were replaced with different shrewd bureaucrats. The swamp Trump drained was replaced with a different swamp. Only the new swamp had the name "Trump" emblazoned upon it in grand gold letters. The American people felt it was time for a radical change, just in a different radical direction.

Madame President Alexandria Ocasio-Cortez was sworn in January 2025, and along with her a wave of like-minded politicians. Within two months, a crisis was manufactured and the Constitution with all the rights recognized by it was suspended for being racist. The regime of Equity was declared, and Ocasio-Cortez simultaneously declared the First Among Equals. People opposed to the new, more tolerant regime headed by FAE Ocasio-Cortez were rounded up given mandatory reeducation holidays. These holidays were to massive camps surrounded with barbed wire and trigger-happy armed guards. The only way out was through lobotomy, figuratively or literally. The America that Donald Trump had presided over was no more, and anyone who so much as deigned to notice the change was swiftly scooped up by the FBI, now the FAE's personal enforcement squad, never to be seen or mentioned of again. All one could do was laugh, but not out loud, as that was considered "triggering" and "problematic," worthy of reeducation.

Equity demanded more and more from the American people (who were no longer called Americans as that was offensive, but simply "folx"). Since those with families fared better than those without, the family unit was abolished. It was forbidden to notice or mention anything that made one person unique compared to another, for such things could produce bias in a person, and Equity forbade such things. One could not recognize the color of another's skin, the sex of a person, how tall or how old a person was, or even if that person was attractive or not. Soon names were abolished since one could show bias to one name or another. All folx were to be called "Citizen" and referred to as such. The only grace Equity allowed was each folx could choose their own pronoun as long as it wasn't "he" or "she." FAE Ocasio-Cortez, who obviously was exempt from the demands of Equity and thus retained her name and identity, ruled the folx forever after. By all authorized accounts it was a true Golden Age. All folx loved her.

They had no choice.

THE END

To see what would've happened if Trump had received his comeuppance earlier, TURN TO PAGE 85.

THANK YOU!

If you enjoyed *A Presidents Day Carol*, you will be excited to learn there is more to discover!

Extra online content for *A Presidents Day Carol*, including Easter eggs and extended scenes, can be found at:
www.ericmhamilton.com/carol-extras/

Check out previous books in this series of United States Presidents with weird sci-fi/fantasy twists.
Franklin Pierce in Death of a Vice President is a gothic tale of murder, madness, and mystery!
An Inconvenient Presidency is a time-travel misadventure of President Al Gore as he relives his presidency over and over again.

For the latest information on all current and upcoming fiction books and other short stories by Eric M. Hamilton, visit his website:
www.ericmhamilton.com

Please leave a review of this book at your favorite online retailer. It is the best way to help independent publishers spread the word!

ABOUT THE AUTHOR

Eric M. Hamilton was born in a land that does not exist, raised in the Midwestern United States, and currently resides in Athens, Alabama with his wife and two children. Eric spends most of his time fighting off feral dinosaurs with his son and dancing to nursery rhymes with his daughter. Occasionally he writes.

CONTENTS